Sue Hendra & Paul Linnet

Oh, Christmas Tree!

MACMILLAN CHILDREN'S BOOKS

On Sidney Street at Christmas time there's magic in the air —

windows bright with twinkly lights and sparkles everywhere.

At 31 the tree is huge,

at 32 it's pink!

At 33 it's very tall and classy, don't you think?

But why no tree at this house?
No wreath upon the door?
Whatever can be going on
at number 34?

There should be decorations
when Christmas time arrives.
So why is it that in this house . . .

Is it a bird?

Is it a cat?

Is it a monster?

Is it a hat?

Who could be chasing them?
What could it be?

Well, blow me down . . .

. . . it's a Christmas tree!

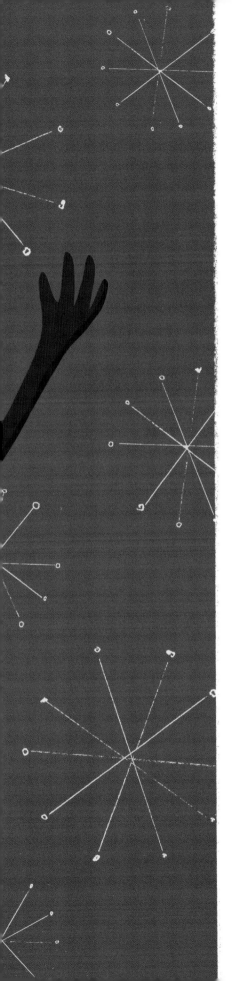

Into the kitchen
the whole lot go racing –
but hang on . . .
the *tree* isn't doing the chasing!

"Sssssstop!" hisses Tinsel.
"Can we talk?" calls out Belle.
"Slow down," pleads Bauble.
"Don't make me yell."

"You're not fooling anyone."

"What's all this about?"

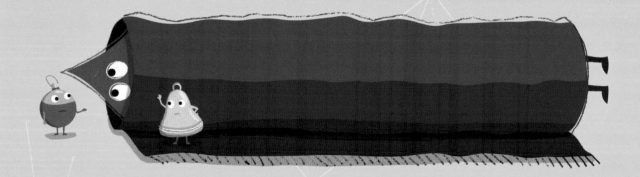 

But Tree carried on,
"I'm not here, I've gone out."

Now Bauble was fuming. "Why can't you see? We're tree decorations and YOU are our tree!

We've all had enough. Why won't you stand still? Just get in that pot — you know the drill!"

"There's been some confusion,"
Tree knelt down and said,
"I'm not standing around
with a star on my head!

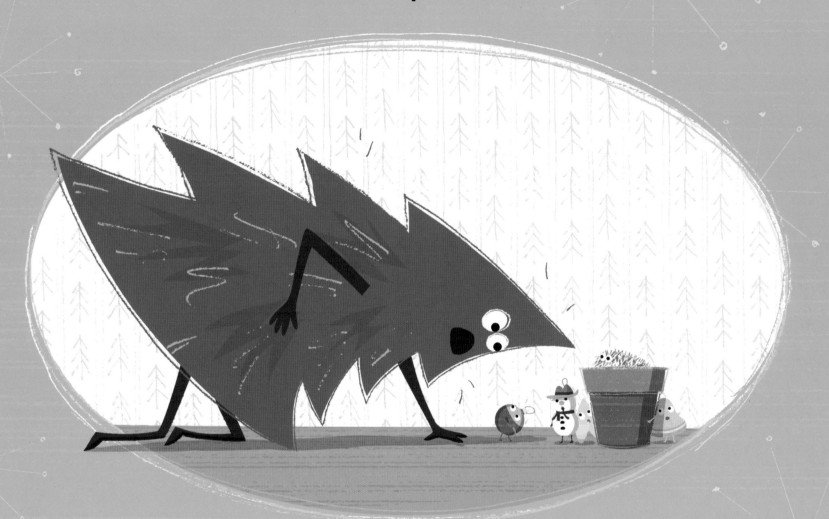

I don't want to be dressed up.
I want to be free!
Now I have to be going
so please excuse me."

"I'd rather be baking,

I love to keep fit.

And sometimes I watch the TV for a bit.

Science is gripping,

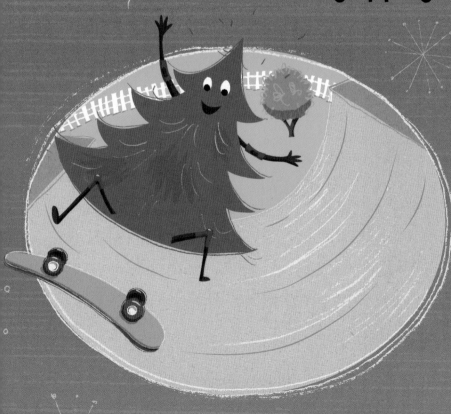

and skating is great . . .

... but to stand in a pot
looking sparkly,
I'd hate!"

Bauble was livid.
"I think that you're rotten!
Christmas is special,
it can't be forgotten!

The tree was confused now,
and somewhat surprised.
"I didn't come here
to be **criticised!**

Enough of this nonsense,
prepare for some shocks . . .

"I truly love Christmas —
it's awesome,
it ROCKS!

I'll be helping with lunch,
I'm both willing and able.
I bet that they'll make me
the head of the table.

And then there's the crackers,
I do love a riddle!
And those colourful hats
that they hide in the middle.

But it's being together
with family and friends
that makes Christmas special
and sad when it ends."

And that was when Belle
had her crafty brainwave . . .

"Dear Tree, we *do* have
a present for you.
I think you deserve it,
the others do too!"

"A present for me?
Oh, I'd like that a LOT!
Now pop off and get it.
Go on . . . off you trot!"

When they came back
Tree was shouting, "Yippee!!!
What is it? What is it?
What can it be??"

"We just know that you'll love it,
we don't mean to gloat."

"You were right!
How fantastic!
New boots, hat,
and coat!

I'm so warm and so cosy,
I love it,
I do!"

"And now I can take part in winter sports too!

I'll be sledging,

and skiing,

carve statues of ice.

And a trek to the North Pole,
now that would be nice!

I'm sorry that you
couldn't decorate me.
But it just couldn't happen,
I'm not that sort of tree!

I've been nothing but trouble —
that much is true.
You should show me the door
without further ado."

Bauble stepped forward,
"You're one of a kind.
You haven't annoyed us,
we really don't mind."

The others all grinned
at Belle's clever coat stunt . . .

For the back of the coat
didn't quite match the front!